Treasure of the Sea

Erotic Short Story

Raven Flanagan

For Anna Kate and all the loving help she provided for this fun short story.

Contents

Treasure of the Sea

Part One

In a world of strange creatures and wild oddities, there is nothing out of the norm. When you live day to day not knowing what life will throw your way, there's no telling what to expect.

My day started normally, like any other day for me and those who stay out of the way.

From the vantage of my seaside home, I was quickly reminded not to stare directly across the water. For in the distance blazed the sun, shining gold, shimmering light that reflected along the vast expanse of emerald and sapphire sea.

While dressing in an airy white sundress, I knew a small fishing boat waited in the cove for me. The same boat of old brown wood, with barnacles underneath that I could map like the stars above, for I knew them so well.

My father had fished in this sea. His parents fished in it before him, just as their parents had. Generations of watching the flying creatures of the sky, massive scaled beasts or feathered monsters. Decades of spotting the serpents of the sea cresting their heads above the far away waves, emerging from within the deepest depths of the oceans.

"Don't go there," Papa always warned. "Our boats aren't made for the deep, and neither are we."

So, every day I took the lonely winding path to the cove, got in my little boat, and set sail to fish the shallows. Here the water was so clear and so vibrant, one could see the pale sand below and all the colorful fish darting about within.

It was a simple life, to sit back and watch the strong gallivant off to insane adventures while I steered my boat and hauled up my nets. In the afternoon, I sold my excess catch to the patrons of the nearby village. The people here were content to sit on the sidelines while heroes fought the monsters.

I sold fish listening to the tales of the day. Some up-and-coming knight slayed a dragon. A prince rescued his beloved princess from a tower. A group of adventurers stopped a wizard from bringing eternal night to the world.

A simple life in a chaotic world.

It was fine with me.

Each night, I would return to my empty home. I would cook, clean, and bathe, washing the sea water from my golden-brown skin. Every day was the same in my lonely life.

I climbed into my boat, stopping as that last thought repeated itself in my head.

Lonely. Hm. I had never had that thought before.

Was I? I asked myself as I took the oars in my hands and rowed out. Am I lonely?

Further and further, my boat went out to the

shallow fish feeding ground. As I rowed, I turned over my mind to identify the origin of the newfound thought.

Eventually, I stopped and tossed out my net. In the cove, I was safe. In the cove, I could let my little boat drift as my thoughts did the same. The gentle rippling of the water soothed me. The same motion I'd known since I was big enough for Papa to bring me along.

The boat swayed. I turned my face up to the massive golden orb in the sky, soaking up the glorious warmth and the cooling breeze from the sea as my newfound curiosity wormed itself back into the forefront of my mind.

Was I lonely?

Most women my age were already married and starting families. Even before my parents had passed, they encouraged me to stay away from the heroes and knights. Instead, they wished for me to find a normal man in the village to settle down with. "Bring him back home and start a new generation of fishermen."

But I had no interest in the men of the village. I'd never felt connected to them or pulled to them in any meaningful way. All those years I believed myself content to go on fishing alone. I was happy enough with the menial tasks of my life.

I woke up. I fished. I ate. I slept. The next day, I did it all again.

But last night had been different, I couldn't deny. Last night, I saw something in the village I shouldn't have seen. Something I'd never seen before. Not between people.

I knew everyone did it. The birds and the bees and everything in between. It was nature, and it was so much more.

Just remembering it, my face heated. Oh my, I shouldn't have seen that.

Under a black sky with silver twinkling stars, I made my way home after selling my fish. I'd turned a corner in the darkness of night. On my otherwise normal journey, I heard something. The rustling of clothes and panting breaths. Around a corner in an alley between buildings, for the first time in my life, I saw two people tangled together in the throes of passion. A man and woman rutting against the back of the tavern.

And I... some part of me... hidden deep in a place that I didn't know existed until then... that part of me wanted. I wanted to be that woman, arching against her partner with a lewd smile on her lips as he pounded her repeatedly. They barely suppressed their increasing moans until they found some rapturous release together.

I'd gone home gasping, face flushed, reeling from what I had seen.

In some respects, I suppose I was indeed lonely.

My boat rocked suddenly, veering to the left. Eyes snapping open as it jerked me from my memories, I realized that I'd drifted too far out while fantasizing. Daydreaming about myself in that woman's position had stolen my focus, and now my boat was cresting over waves increasing.

Heading toward the deep.

On the horizon, where the water had turned as dark as midnight, a massive serpent broke the surface.

"Oh, no." I reared back, grasping for one of my oars.

My hand hit the wood, knocking my right oar from my fingers. It fell into the water, floating away in the waves too far to reach. A splash in the water made me look around, but this far from the cove I couldn't see what swam under the surface. A stirring in the water made my heart spike with fear.

Entirely distracted, I'd gone too far. Now I was in trouble.

The monster's green and red head erupted from the surface. A high-pitched scream escaped me as the sea-serpent rose higher and higher, its long neck never ending. Its massive head and maw, full of dagger-like teeth, blocked out the afternoon sun.

I wasn't one of the damsels in distress who the villagers would delight in telling tales of. There would be no princes or knights coming to save me. Not in my world. Not in my story.

No, I was a nobody who never got to experience the excitement of life and a sea-beast was going to eat me. A rather exciting end to an otherwise monotonous life. Though an otherwise funny idea, the irony of my present situation was rather humorless at the moment as I stared into the hungry mouth of the creature that would surely be the only witness to my final breath.

Those teeth aimed for me, a salivating maw gaping wide and ready for a bite. Its endless black eyes bore into, targeting its easy prey. The screams from my lips never stopped. My heart dropped into gut and—

Another creature, as dark and as beautiful as the richest emerald in the world, surged from the waves. Long waves of black hair streamed behind the body. Frills and fins lined the incredibly muscular figure. Finishing out the unearthly form was a tail, long and streamlined for perfect maneuvers under the water.

All this I caught in that brief glimpse, all ten feet of that wonderful creature.

A creature with a spear in its hand.

The sea serpent jerked its head back as that spear sliced across an eye. An ear-splitting shriek bellowed out from the depths of the monster's open jaws, frilled head writhing up from the sea in its moment of pain. The action sent tall waves sweeping my miniscule boat further out into the ocean.

The human-adjacent sea creature exploded from the waves again. This time, the spear plunged not into an eye, but the space on the serpent's head right between them.

One last rumbling scream shook the water. The serpent's gargantuan body slammed into the waves. The resounding force rocked my unsteady boat violently over and over as the monster sank.

At the last moment, the monster's tail hit my

boat. The wood shattered apart around me, breaking into shards of wood and splinters.

I dropped into the water, my cry for help bubbling away on my lips.

I'm going to die. I'm alone and I'm going to die in the water that's always been my second home. I'm going to die in the same water where I was raised, taught to fish, and swam my entire life.

My legs kicked, and my arms flailed. I mustered every ounce of my strength, but the water was too strong. I couldn't fight the overwhelming current of the immense serpent's body sinking and sucking everything down with it.

There wasn't enough air in my lungs, and they ached with the need to take a breath. The daylight faded as my vision went black. One last bubble of air escaped my lips as my exhausted body descended the murky waves of the deep—

A hard body crashed into mine under the waves.

Currents of water rushed past me. The next thing I knew, my head was cresting over the waves. The next thing I knew, my head was cresting over the waves. Likely because of the mysterious force that had collided with me, I was now far away from the roiling water where the serpent sank below. Though, how such a force could move so quickly in what seemed such a short amount of time was beyond me.

Powerful arms caged me against a hard body, keeping my head above the unabating water. My eyes fluttered open against the sea spray on my face to catch the side profile of the other creature.

My breath caught in my throat.

He didn't have the face of a frightening creature, as I might have expected. Instead, he possessed the face of a devastatingly handsome male. Sharp-angled features that spoke of strength and power. The face of a man that any maiden would fall for.

But he was no man. He was more than any human male could ever dream of being. Long finned ears stuck out from his damp, wavy black hair. His pale skin held a slight green shimmer. There were three slits on the sides of his neck that mirrored gills on a fish. The hands that held me close had sharp claws and webbing between the fingers.

I'd heard stories of his kind. In the moments before we vanished into a seaside cave, I realized what he was.

This was a merman.

I knew this cave. It was part of the cove I've fished out of. I'd explored this place many times as a young girl.

The mouth of the cave was large enough to let in the afternoon light. The water here became increasingly shallow and still. Only our approach caused a stirring in the crystal-clear waters. Toward the back of the cave was a sandy clearing between the rocky outcroppings.

The merman took me as far as he could in the water. Once we reached the shallows, he stopped, setting me down. My bottom landed on the sandy floor as water lapped around my waist.

All the water had soaked into my dress, clinging to my drenched body like a second skin. My pebbled nipples strained against the fabric. For a moment, I might have imagined the feeling of someone staring at my chest.

A warm, wet hand cupped my cheek, pulling my face up. I gasped openly at the striking ocean blue gaze, staring so deeply into my eyes that it breached my very soul. He smelled of the sea and something distinctly masculine that I couldn't place.

I liked it.

He continued angling my head, and I stopped moving, stopped breathing, as he examined me. As if he was checking me for injuries. I didn't feel any pain, though that might have been from the fiery adrenaline coursing through my body.

Adrenaline. That had to be why my blood sang under my skin. It couldn't have been from those firm, vise-like fingers roaming over my arms, lifting and turning them. It couldn't have been from his body resting between my legs, writhing as he assessed me, pressing on the soft, intimate part of me.

While he looked over me, I took the opportunity to take him in as well. From the insanely sculpted chest and abs to the vibrant green starting at his hips where flesh met... not quite scales, but not exactly the texture of a dolphin. They looked like scales, but I could feel his long fin against my thighs when he moved, and they were smooth and warm.

He scooted down deeper into the water. His

hands trailed over me to my legs. When I felt his thumb press into a sensitive spot on my hip, an undignified squeak slipped from me. My eyes widened at the noise, and he glanced up briefly, curiously staring.

I bit my lip and didn't move. He went back to his examination, touching all over my legs for any sign of whatever it was that he looked for. I admired the length of his lovely green tail almost as a distraction from the touch on my leg.

Dark green, yet vibrant. Glimmering and reflecting light like emeralds. *Gods, he's so beautiful...*

"Ah!" I yelped as he jerked my other leg above the water.

His head snapped up to me, pinched by what I read as concern. He parted his full lips and sighed. When he looked down at my leg again, I noticed the raw, red scrapes on the inside of my thigh just above my knee.

Carefully, he passed his fingers over the wound, and I unwittingly hissed. I hadn't felt that until I'd seen it. Now that I was aware of the wound, I noticed the ache.

"*Hurt.*" It wasn't my language. It was another. A musical language I'd never heard before. And yet when that deep, low voice came from him, I understood him perfectly.

I shouldn't have been able to. I only knew my native tongue.

My head nodded in answer as I lost the ability to

talk. The merman could speak! With that, I knew I had to thank him for saving my life.

Before I knew what was happening, he grabbed my hips and pushed me further up the shallows, until my butt was on damp sand and only my feet remained in the water. The merman followed, slithering through the calm water to settle between my legs again.

I clenched my jaw when he lifted my leg, peering closely at the scrape on it. Part of the broken boat must have hit me when I went under. Who could say how many splinters I had buried in my skin now?

Then he pressed his mouth to my skin. Soft lips on my injury, gently sucking at the flesh. It sent an unusual spark of heat jolting through my body, starting from my core and spreading through my chest.

My leg trembled against him as I whined, "Wait. What are you doing?"

Pulling back, he picked up on the worried tone in my voice. His brows met as he frowned. "*Help. Heal.*" He glanced between me and the wound.

"With—with your mouth?" I asked.

Without speaking again, he nodded enthusiastically. He *wanted* to help me, to heal me.

"Ah... alright." He didn't hesitate to cover my raw skin with his mouth again, sucking on the tender flesh. I held my breath when he pulled back to spit out the splinters.

Once the splinters were sufficiently gone, the merman's long, long—*gods how is it so long*—tongue flicked out to lick at the wound. Each firm press of that slippery, hot tongue over my injured skin eased the slight sting of pain. Something in his saliva must possess healing properties.

However, another part of me burned. It was a strange coiling heat between my legs. At the very center of me, I experienced a rising warmth that I'd felt only a fraction of while watching that couple in the alley the night before. Seeing and feeling this gorgeous merman licking and sucking the inside of my thigh brought a strange haze into my mind that settled over my body.

I was only half aware of my spread legs and my lack of undergarments. My soaked dress, bunched around my waist, exposed the most intimate part of my body, and I was too distracted to care. Not when it felt so good when he licked higher up the inside of my thigh.

Part Two

His nostrils flared suddenly. Those sea-blue eyes whipped up to gawk at me. That's when he looked between my legs. The look he gave me then, accompanied by the increasing grip of his hand holding my thigh, almost frightened me.

My heart rate spiked, fluttering within my chest like the wings of a hummingbird. If I could open my chest, my heart would fly away from me to escape the flaring flames within my body.

That look in his eyes was like nothing I'd ever received from a male before. Yet, I instinctively knew it. His eyes darkened, narrowing on me with pure animal desire.

"*Aroused*," he growled in that deep musical voice. It wasn't a question; merely a simply stated fact.

I didn't know how to respond to that. Without realizing it, my head quickly nodded. Suddenly embarrassed, I attempted to close my legs.

His hands stopped me. In fact, he spread my legs wider apart. I swallowed hard when his gaze traveled along my body to the apex of my legs. Then he licked his lips like a starving man ready to devour the meal before him.

Sea-blue eyes looked up at me again. An

unspoken question swirled in their depths even as he moved closer, lowering his head. But our gazes remained locked, one of his brows rising while waiting for me to agree to something salacious I couldn't yet fathom.

"*Taste*?" he finally asked. I didn't really understand what he meant.

Did he want to taste me... *there*?

My cheeks burned, surely turning as red as a ripe tomato. Everything inside of me heated, my internal temperature increasing as his head lowered. Something throbbed low in my core, telling me I wanted to experience this. No, I needed it.

So, I nodded in agreement, voicing my consent in a small whisper. "Yes."

A rumbling growl from the back of his throat caused me to tense up. Only the sincere warmth in his eyes kept me from trying to escape. The noise vibrated through his chest, making him sound like the primal animal he was.

He came closer to my core, inhaling deeply. My heart thumped harder against my ribs, and he closed the gap. His eyes dilated until they were wholly black, as the scent of my arousal overwhelmed him with an instinct I was only beginning to understand.

"What is happening?" I whispered to myself. All the while watching him, unmoving. One of his massive hands on my thigh spread me further. In doing so, I felt a wetness drip out of me. A slick fluid, the evidence of my increasing wanton thoughts affecting my body.

"*Smell good*," he moaned, inches from my core.

He pulled at my leg with his hard grip under my knee. My breath hitched as I fell back onto my elbows in the sand. Gentle water tickled my feet, but his hot breath fanning my slick pussy stole my entire focus. His wet palm skimmed up my leg, along the tender skin of my inner thigh.

My entire body trembled with a growing fire I wanted to explore. Though this situation was insane and almost unbelievable compared to my ordinary life, I couldn't turn back now.

I wasn't the princess who would be saved from the dragon by her princely lover. No, I was the girl who would be devoured by the sea.

The merman positioned himself between my legs, his long green tail slightly swishing in the shallow water. The sight of him there made my heart leap into my throat.

He was large. More massive than any man I'd ever seen in my life. He could have completely coiled around me like a snake and squished the life out of me if he'd had the thought to do so. Instead, the bare prick of his claws on my thighs held my legs open, making me feel like small prey beneath him.

Unable to wholly grasp what was happening, some unexplored part of me knew the unbridled hunger in his eyes. He inhaled my scent again, his chest heavily rising and falling in a way that mirrored my slow panting. Then the tip of his tongue flicked out, teasing over the sensitive skin on my upper thigh.

My muscles tensed, and my head fell back. The sensual tickle of his tongue rose higher up my skin, licking up the droplets of salty water and tasting my flesh.

Cradling my thighs in his massive hands, the merman's claws almost pricked at my skin. As if conscious of my more delicate nature, he held me tenderly, despite the razor-sharp tips of his webbed hands. This was dangerous, I knew, yet I experienced no fear - only swirling heat.

"Oh!" An indecent whimper broke apart my thoughts as the merman's impossibly long tongue probed at my glistening folds. Exploring gently at first, he lapped up the wetness he found there. That long, flexible tongue moved over me with expert ease.

The vibrations of his pleased growls rippled through the air between us. It was like he was purring at the taste.

It caught me off guard when his tongue passed over a buzzing bead of nerves. It sent me arching up, bucking my hips uncontrollably. A drawn-out moan left me as I shuddered. Tension danced over my tight skin, and my nipples tingled against the damp fabric of my dress.

The merman continued licking and exploring my folds, sucking down the slick fluid of my desire. He wiggled his tongue over my clit repeatedly. It was strange and new, but the sensation was amazing in every way as he pleasured me.

His eyes remained open, observing me and every

brief spasm of my body as he tasted me. His tongue retreated abruptly, and a pitiful noise of complaint slipped out of me. However, he closed the distance, covering my core with his open mouth to suck on my bead of nerves.

Delicious warmth expanded through me, over my limbs. Those sensations caused me to curl my toes and rock my hips into his mouth. My head spun and my heart erratically beat at the alarming pleasure flooding my body.

The merman's hands drifted to my hips, holding my squirming body in place. My throat constricted as the heady combination of his tongue on my core and his hand on my skin drove my head into the clouds.

Withdrawing his tongue from my folds, I took those seconds to gather in a lungful of air, gasping while my head cleared in a moment of brief clarity. I knew that this strange event should terrify me. But it didn't.

"Oh, by the gods," I breathed out, shivering against the cool breeze coming in from the ocean. My mouth opened as if to speak again. Before I could say anything else, his flexible, writhing tongue slipped into my wet, aching entrance with surprising ease.

"Fuck!" I cursed for the first time in my life. Falling back entirely on the sand, I saw stars coming to life behind my closed eyes. His tongue filled me instantly. Thick and warm, alive in a way as it found the deepest, unexplored part of me. When his tongue squirmed, my walls clenched around it.

Those claw-tipped hands on my hips squeezed in return, acknowledging my body's response to his ministrations. He growled with amusement; the sound meeting my ears and echoing without end. That wickedly wild tongue discovered all the places inside of me receptive to pleasure, and he rubbed them repeatedly.

My body and mind succumbed to the heat and the newfound feelings. A powerful storm rose inside of me, something vibrant and glorious. That luscious, roiling heat coiled low in my stomach, building in the softest parts of my core. The pleasure crested higher with each pass of his tongue pumping into me, long enough to fill me entirely and still rub over my clit.

Every fiber of my being burned while he tongue-fucked me. The act intoxicated me more than the plum wine my family used to make. And when that all-encompassing bliss exploded through my belly, out through my limbs, I screamed with a surprising tenacity.

His tongue undulated inside of me while my body trembled. My fingers dug into the sand, fumbling for purchase on anything tangible, reaching for anything to help ground my mind during wave after wave of exhilarating release. That wicked tongue didn't stop wriggling against my pulsing walls until my body finally relaxed into the bright afterglow of my climax.

The feeling of his thick, firm tongue slithering

out of me was almost enough to make me come again. Even so, I slumped into the sand, feeling the merman's hands vanish from my hips.

What just happened?

Through my eyelids, a darkness blocked the drifting sunset. Eyes snapping open, I looked up in time to see the merman crawling over my body. The air froze in my lungs as his heated weight settled between my legs more intimately than the first time.

"*Good*?" He rumbled with a voice like harmonic thunder.

"I'm good. It was good. Very good." A shy smile spread over my quivering lips. A chasm opened in my chest upon witnessing the possessive darkness and never-ending hunger lingering in his eyes.

"Do you... Do you have a name?" I forced the words out, unsure of what to say. "I'm Scylla."

"Scylla," he repeated in my language. His startling blue eyes locked onto my gaze, holding me in place as he studied every little detail of my face, from my rich brown eyes to the brown hair curling around my face, highlighted from years under the sun. I could have sworn he noted each wayward freckle scattered over my nose and cheeks.

Bracing himself on one elbow, he placed a hand over his chest, drawing my eyes to his tensing abdominal muscles. His fingers splayed, showing off the delicate webbing between them. "*Aearadan. Name.*"

"Thank you for saving me, Aearadan. I appreciate it." And I appreciated the thing with the tongue...

"*Will always save,*" he asserted. That pulled my wandering eyes back to his face. A sudden seriousness lurking in his eyes made me freeze. "*Watch Scylla for many moons.*"

"Oh," I added stupidly. This merman had been watching me. Was he looking out for me?

"*See Scylla fishing alone. Alone for long time.*" His palm cupped my cheek, and I sucked in a breath. His lips mimicked a smile, reigniting my heart to race again. "*Not alone now.*"

"No. I'm not alone now, am I?" The urge to weep pricked at the back of my eyes. A storm of emotions I couldn't yet untangle swarmed my chest, but I tamped them down into silence for now.

Reaching up, I wrapped my fingers around his wrist to pull his hand from my face. His expression fell for a second. Until he realized where I placed his hand. Down my neck to my chest, I placed his large palm over my dress onto my breast.

This indecent courage building inside of me motivated me to keep going. Without expressing it, I knew Aearadan wanted me. I knew he wanted more from me. I wanted the same things.

My voice took a husky tone I didn't recognize when I spoke again. "Would you like a reward for saving me?"

Ordinary Scylla never would have asked for such a ludicrous thing. But right now, that girl was gone. In her place was a wanton woman, spreading her legs for the merman who was grinding against her with each sway of his tail.

"*Scylla want Aearadan?*" He sounded amazed at the concept, surprised even that I would desire him. His stare remained on my chest, watching enrapt as I allowed him the opportunity to massage my round breast.

Due to his stimulating touch, I couldn't help but to moan the simplest of responses. "Yes."

When his hand pulled away, I moved swiftly. In a blur, I grasped the bunched-up dress around my waist and lifted it over my head. I tossed the soaked white fabric somewhere behind me and turned my attention back to the merman.

"*Aearadan want Scylla,*" he rasped, the sound full of agony and longing. His eyes seared into my flesh, gazing at every inch of my exposed skin. Seeing his lips part as his jaw dropped made me feel like a goddess.

"*Reward?*" Aearadan shook his head, not content with that word. His brows creased as the corner of his mouth fell. While his eyes roamed my body, a new glimmer shone in his eyes, bringing out a new smile. "*Treasure.*"

Aearadan's head dipped out of nowhere. His long tongue swept across my chest, flicking over one nipple and then the next. I collapsed into the sand again, hips rolling against his groin and the two pelvic fins there.

"*Delicious treasure,*" he groaned from deep within his chest.

His mouth converged on a breast. My head arched back at the jolt from my breast to my core. The tip of his tongue teased my hardened nipple within his mouth. He held my breasts, pushing them together to better lick and suck them. All the while, the heavy weight of his body rubbing between my thighs drove me wild.

Even with my returning desire and the needy tension connecting us, I wondered what would happen. I was familiar enough with male anatomy to know that Aearadan needed a specific part for what I believed might come next. Only slippery skin pressed against my pussy. While that grinding motion was indeed amazing, it wasn't enough.

"Aearadan, how can we—" a sudden buck from his hips shut me up. He groaned against my skin, influenced by his name on my lips.

"Aearadan." I repeated his name, and he pushed his groin against me harder. This time, something new wriggled between us.

Glancing down, Aearadan lifted to readjust. In the space between our bodies, I noticed a new appendage unfurling from a previously hidden slit between his pelvic fins. My jaw dropped at the girthy length of his tapered cock.

Chills raced over my arms when a second one appeared. The swirling shades of green on his cocks mesmerized me, eliciting a fresh wave of growing desire inside of me. I swallowed over the pooling saliva in my mouth.

Two. Oh, by the gods. He has TWO!

Whatever happened next, I trusted him. This merman had saved my life and kissed my core in a way that gave me astounding pleasure for the first time in my life. Aearadan would take me as a man takes a woman, and I'd rejoice in our joining with my whole being.

"*Small*," he hummed, "*soft*." A feral grin graced his sensual lips, twisting my stomach with a craving for more.

Tentatively, my trembling hands rose to his shoulders. The curtain of his dark hair fell around us as Aearadan settled into place over me. His long tail extended into the water, and he aligned his first cock with my wet pussy.

I shuddered, gasping lightly when his cock rubbed against me. His dick was slick, as if his body produced its own lubrication. My nails clung to his shoulders, but with his thicker skin, Aearadan didn't seem to notice. He merely threw his head back, groaning with animalistic delight as he ground his shaft against me.

Aearadan lowered onto his elbows. My hands traveled from his shoulders, down his solid chest to his muscled stomach, tensing at my feather light touch. His entire body was lean muscle, hardened to survive the struggles of life in the dangerous seas. Every part of him screamed of predatory beauty.

"Scylla." His strained voice made me blink up at him. Suddenly locked in his blue eyes, I read the conflict in his gaze. Aearadan wanted me, but he didn't want to hurt me.

"It's alright. We'll be alright." With my new conviction to see this through, I reached between us and grabbed the cock slipping between my lower lips. A surprised hiss slipped between his teeth. His sounds quickly became a breathy groan when I angled him at my entrance and tilted my hips.

The tapered tip of his cock slipped inside me with astounding ease. Like breathing, it came naturally for my body to welcome Aearadan. His lubed cock and my relaxed, eager pussy joined like fitting puzzle pieces.

"Oh, gods!" My head fell back as I cried out. Aearadan stretched me delightfully, filling me one slow inch at a time.

Something in his language burst from his lips. I couldn't understand him at that time, but it sounded like a curse. He buried his face against my throat, breathing hard, with his lips hovering against my skin. His massive body trembled with barely contained restraint.

This beast wanted to rut me into the sand with all the power in this body. Yet, for my sake, he held back on what he was capable of. After seeing this body leap impossibly high from the waves and take down a sea serpent, I knew he could undoubtedly tear me in half.

"*Watch Scylla for so long*," he admitted again. "*Want Scylla for so long*."

For many moons, Aearadan had said he'd watched me. Were those many moons' months or years? How long had this merman watched me when I went fishing in the cove? How had I never noticed him before?

In any other situation, that might have frightened me. Right now, it made me feel that in all that time since my parents passed, I hadn't truly been as alone as I believed. Someone had been there with me, watching and caring for me even if I didn't know it.

Now he was inside of me.

"Why did you want me? Why did you watch me, Aearadan?" I'm not sure why I chose that moment to ask. That moment when his cock filled me with as much as my smaller stature could endure. He froze, remaining in place and allowing me a moment to adjust to the intense stretching.

Before answering, his tongue flicked out against my neck. A wild shiver ran through my body, making my nipples tingle and my cunt clench on his cock. He purred with male pride at my body's reactions.

"*Scylla family came from sea long ago. Great-great-grandmother sea-woman fall in love with male on land. Clan keep watch over our kind.*"

All at once, my body sank into the sand as every thought in my mind went haywire. Some of the delicious sexual haze in my head cleared upon hearing Aearadan's admission.

"My ancestor was a mermaid?" I openly balked, drowning in his blue ocean eyes. "Oh, gods, I didn't know."

"*Ah, sorry for say—*" Aearadan moved to get off me as he noticed the rising panic in my features.

At the feeling of his cock slipping out, I wrapped

my arms around his neck to stop him. "No, no, wait. It's alright. I'm—I'm just surprised. We can keep going if you want."

The extent of my desire was unbearable and now that he was inside of me, I needed to continue. It was foolish, but I could face the news of my lineage later. Right now, my focus was on feeling that exploding warmth in my belly again and experiencing it with Aearadan.

"*Want* Scylla. *Very bad want* Scylla," Aearadan lamented. "*Not supposed to want* Scylla."

To spur him on, I wiggled my hips, pushing them up to meet him. I held my breath, as did he, while he followed the urge to enter me again. Ignoring the conversation that would come after, I allowed my body and mind to melt into that sensual heat.

Careful and slow, Aearadan went as deep as he could, touching on the parts of me that only he knew now. My hands circled around his waist when he pulled out. I skimmed my fingers over the area where his tough skin met smooth scales, admiring the surprising inner warmth of his body.

"You can have me, Aearadan. It's okay. You can have me." Moaning from each delicious thrust, my eyes closed, and I became encompassed by the momentous act we shared. Writhing together, moving as if we were one single being, sharing primal pleasure.

Registering my words, Aearadan emitted a frightening growl. A possessive snarl tore from his lips at the same time he flattened his body flush to mine. It crushed the air from my lungs, but gods, I loved it. His body, fully covering and squeezing my own, allowed my lust-addled brain to vanish into a soothing darkness.

"*Mine now,*" he asserted. The pure dominance in his musical baritone washed over me, settling into my bones as an undeniable fact. In some way I couldn't yet grasp, Aearadan had laid claim to me.

Each thrust of his cock brought us closer together. Closer to finding the sweet release we craved. And with each thrust, his second cock brushed against my behind. It was strange, but it made my cheeks redden as a reminder of this momentous moment.

"Yours," I blindly agreed. His mouth slammed into mine, silencing anything else I might have said.

Clumsily at first, we explored one another's mouths. Sloppily kissing, thanks to my inexperience. Aearadan didn't seem to mind. Instead, he used his lips and the motion of his mouth to guide me.

He kissed my top lip, then my bottom. His actions were near agonizing with how slow and tender they were. That is, until his slithering tongue parted my lips wide and delved into my mouth. I choked on a gasp as his tongue tangled with mine, and I tasted the sea on his lips.

I curled my arms over his ribs, careful of the gills there that mirrored the smaller ones on his neck. Aearadan's heart beat inside of his chest so hard that I felt it echoed in mine. When my legs lifted to wrap around his hips, that pounding heart rate spiked.

With my legs secured around his waist, it forced Aearadan to make less of a pounding motion and more of a grinding one. This wholly shocked me as he ground against my clit with each rock of his hips. My breath hitched at the electrifying pleasure scattering all over my body in response.

Aearadan smiled into my mouth, sharing my breath. Perceiving the motion that had produced such a reaction from me, he increased his efforts. Grinding harder into me each time, his thick, pliable cock entered me. Breathy, embarrassing noises ran away from me, and the merman smirked wickedly knowing he caused them.

His cock rubbing those sensitive places inside of me as he ground himself against my pearl of pleasure drove my head into the clouds. Aearadan's tongue extended from his lips, laving over my neck as my head arched back. The exploring tongue swirled over my chest, down to my breasts. It twirled over a peaked nipple, forcing erotic flames to burst through me.

His attention to my breast added to the tightness in my core. This time, when the coiling warmth went taut inside my belly, I knew what would happen next. So, I embraced that inflamed pleasure between my thighs, growing higher with each drive of his girth splitting me apart.

"Oh, Aearadan!" That tight string holding me together snapped. I fell apart at the seams. My second climax rushed through me, shaking my entire body.

Aearadan hissed through his teeth, clenching his jaw. As my pussy pulsed around his cock, his hips jerked, and his breathing picked up. Before I knew what was happening, something warm gushed through me, filling me to the brim.

Bliss simmered through my blood. Aearadan nearly collapsed onto me, catching himself before utterly crushing me with his weight. I wouldn't have minded if he had.

Catching me off guard, Aearadan curled his clawed fingers over my arms, then rolled over. I yelped with surprise as we spun over the sand. His cock withdrew, and I shuddered.

Aearadan laid back, and I found myself splayed across his chest, straddling his tail. One of his hands urged my head to lie down. With my ear to his skin, I heard the erratic thundering of his heart, berating in time with mine.

There was no telling how long we laid there embracing each other. The sun drifted across the horizon, out across the sea. Gulls cried from somewhere in the cove, and the lapping waves became a soothing song.

The only thing that didn't change was the hardness of Aearadan against my behind. My face remained flushed with heat, and my heart refused to stop racing.

Was he not sated? I felt his seed dripping out of me and wondered if he had more to give. Could Aearadan fill me again and again?

Without saying a word, I braced myself on his chest. I found Aearadan intently watching me. When I looked up, he held his breath. His eyes went back and forth between mine, and I got the feeling he had something to say.

"You said that you're not supposed to want me, but you do. Why?" As I spoke, I sat up. Aearadan's cock twitched against my ass, yet we both seemed to ignore it.

"*Scylla family leave sea. Watch over, but not supposed to interact. Long ago grandmother banished for love of human.*" He sighed. The sound devastated me. "*I watch Scylla. Sad girl. Beautiful girl. But sad.*"

Aearadan's hand lifted, skimming his knuckles over my cheek. I leaned into that touch, drawn to him like a magnet. "*Fall in love with sad, beautiful girl.*" His features twisted with agony. "*Boat drift out too far. Had to save.*"

Love.

My brows shot up to my forehead, and my heart did somersaults against my chest. Did I hear that right? He really must have been watching me for a long time for those deep emotions to take root.

That hand on my face dropped. I missed the warmth of his hand until he placed it over my breast, over my heart, beneath. His muscles tensed and his cock twitched again, but his steady gaze remained on my eyes alone.

"*Scylla heart calls for the sea. Aearadan can't ignore song.*" He swiftly grabbed my wrist and placed my hand over his heart.

Our hearts beat at the same time.

I inhaled sharply, flinching away. Aearadan held tight to my wrist, keeping my palm over his heart, and his on mine.

"*Heart song.*"

After a breath that lasted an eternity, I repeated, "Heart song."

Part Three

Aearadan relaxed, releasing my wrist. Content with watching me, he laid back in the sand, tucking his arms behind his head in a way that made his muscles bulge deliciously.

My pussy throbbed at the naughty thought accompanying the view. Those sea-blue eyes turned stormy. Glancing down, he noted my bare pussy, dripping his seed on his lower abdomen where flesh met tail. A hint of a proud grin graced those lips.

Suddenly embarrassed, a feeling made worse by the knowledge he had shared, I climbed off Aearadan's tail. To distract myself, I ran my hands down the length of his tail fin. Ignoring the two cocks still proudly jutting forward, I traced the patterns of his flat, scale-like skin. A soft, rumbling purr vibrated through his chest as I admired the beauty in the rich green coloring.

The tip of his frilled fins splashed from the shallow water. Unbeknownst to me, a wide smile pulled my lips. Seeing Aearadan, a merman, in his full glory, filled my heart with a glimmering light. It made me feel like I was seeing the sun for the first time after living my whole life in darkness.

I'd known his kind existed. Of course, living and

working on the sea, everyone in the village knew of their existence. Finding out my ancestor was one of them, a woman who left the sea for the love of a human? Now that was a surprise.

No one ever said anything. Perhaps by the time I was born, everyone had forgotten. A touch of the sea lingered in our blood, but my family had ignored the pull to return. Instead, we set out on the boat, sitting atop the waves, day after day... so close to our true home.

"You say I'm beautiful, but your tail is akin to the most vibrant gemstones I've ever laid my eyes on." Petting his tail, I looked back at his face. He'd gone up on his elbows, observing me as I touched the length of him. "You're exquisite, Aearadan."

Aearadan shook his head, eyes closing. I settled on my knees near his pelvic fins, trying not to look between them. When he opened his sea-storm eyes again, Aearadan reached out.

"*Scylla most beautiful.*" The tips of his fingers ran through my unruly hair. Wild curls bounced around my face because of the drying ocean water. Aearadan touched my hair, carefully twirling a strand around his clawed finger over the webbing.

"*Scylla mine.*" The merman's assertive tone sparked something in the primal center of my being. The simple yet possessive statement leashed around my heart and tugged it closer to his.

"I suppose I am now," I agreed. It felt right to say it. "Yes, I am yours."

Unable to pause and think about what that

meant for my future, something in the corner of my eye snared my attention. Angling my head to the side, I noticed the weeping tips of Aearadan's cocks. Both of his thick members were straining and unyielding.

My hand moved on its own. I grasped the first cock that had been inside of me. Aearadan hissed in pleased surprise at the contact. He shivered from head to tail as my hand stroked from the thicker base to the tapered tip.

An idea formed in my head - one that came to life on its own and moved through me. Leaning forward, I parted my lips and took his cock in my mouth.

I didn't know what I was doing, only that I wanted to do this.

Aearadan sucked in a gasp, bucking his hips when my lips covered his cock. The action drove him further into my mouth and I struggled to swallow the extra length. But I pressed on after seeing his reaction.

Mimicking his thrusting inside of me, I rose and fell on his length... at least, all that would fit to the back of my throat. My tongue swept over the shaft with each pass, licking up the salty, masculine flavor of his slick cock.

From the corner of my eye, I spied the second cock. I couldn't leave that one wanting. I freed a hand and grasped it. One in my mouth and the other in my hand, I sucked and stroked Aearadan's dicks in tandem.

He undulated his hips, meeting the motion of my hand and mouth. Increasing growls, a predatory song, erupted from deep within his chest as I pleasured him.

More sticky fluid seeped from the tips, correctly proving my thought that his members were self-lubricating. I felt it slipping between my hand and the smooth skin of his cock and coating my tongue as I sucked him off. I swallowed and swallowed and swallowed every inch I could, compelling my throat over the tip to hum my satisfaction on the girthy member.

"*Scylla.*" Aearadan snarled my name. A shiver instinctively raced up my spine at the beastly sound. Popping off his length, I looked up at him. A long string of his sticky fluid and my bubbling saliva connected my lips to his twitching cock. More of it dribbled down my chin onto my breasts.

His line of sight followed it. He snarled again.

By now, the golden orb of the sun had dipped half into the sea. Beyond our secluded cave, the water blackened from the draining light. Streaks of purple, red, and yellow stained the edges of the horizon as the dome of the sky darkened. The first stars flickered to light, and the crescent moon eased in to take away the last of the day.

Even in the dim cave, I couldn't escape those glimmering, vibrant blue eyes. They shone with an inner glow of their own, reflecting every ounce of the light in the cave. Maybe it helped him see in the blackest, deepest part of the sea where no sun penetrated.

Aearadan lurched forward, snatching me by the arms. I squeaked with surprise but fell into his embrace. He pulled me over his chest, diving forward to claim my mouth with his. This time, I met his kiss with a touch more skill.

His tongue swept into my mouth, tasting our combined flavors. My tongue flicked into his. This made Aearadan push his mouth harder into mine with near bruising intensity. It made my head swim, and I gladly drowned in the feeling.

A fresh wave of that newly familiar burning hunger blossomed between my thighs. Despite the faint ache in my core, an instinct unlike any other drove me into Aearadan's embrace again. I tossed my leg over his tail, straddling his hips while our kisses deepened.

Knowing what to do now, how to take my pleasure and what I wanted from him, I lifted my hips. Bracing my knees in the sand on either side of his hips, I angled myself to meet his cock. His body tensed when I grabbed his length, yet he didn't halt the kiss.

That purring in his chest encouraged me to keep going. I aimed his tip at my entrance. I rubbed my pussy over his shaft, spreading my liquid arousal and his fluid. Some part of me wanted to tease him with what was to come, I suppose.

I couldn't wait long. Without another second to spare, I pushed myself down onto his cock. Gritting my teeth at the sudden intrusion, I breathed in to steady myself. Aearadan moaned against my lips, easing my grinding teeth until I opened for another kiss.

It took me a moment to breathe through it. Nevertheless, I sank myself down onto the first few inches of his cock. This time, when he filled me, his second cock poked at me from behind.

My eyes widened nearly to the size of dinner plates. Aearadan stilled underneath me. Our faces parted, and he gazed up at me, both of us frozen from that brief contact.

His second cock settled between my cheeks, throbbing with heat. My walls clenched on the first cock sliding inside me as the second one twitched against my behind.

The idea forming in my head was taboo for humans, though I didn't think it mattered. And right now, it seemed like an act I'd greatly like to try.

I'm already fucking a merman. How much further could I go?

I didn't break contact with his searing, questioning stare. I held my gaze with Aearadan, hovering over his hips as I reached blindly behind me. A muscle in his jaw twitched, and a line formed between his brows the instant my fingers curled over his second cock.

Aearadan's nostrils flared, and he swallowed whatever growling noise rose in his chest. He braced his hands on my thighs, barely containing his claws digging into my soft flesh.

Taking a deep breath, I released the tension in

my body. I loosened my muscles and prepared to welcome a second appendage. I pushed the second cock forward and sank another few inches.

The tapered tip of the second cock, coated in his body's natural lubricant, probed my ass. My body inherently tensed up at the sudden intrusion, squeezing the tip as if to push him back out.

Through it all, Aearadan remained perfectly still. He watched, patiently waiting to see what I would do. His claws dug into my thighs and an unhinged hiss slipped from him.

"Scylla."

"Is this alright?" I'd managed another inch when he said my name. Worried, I read his expression for any sign that he wanted me to stop.

"*Tight. Good tight.*" He closed his eyes, head falling into the sand. Luscious waves of long black hair fanned around his head, showing off the green tipped fins at the point of his ears.

Gods, he's so beautiful. And right now, I have this large, handsome merman at my mercy. He's moaning and breathing hard because of me. I want more of that. I want to make him feel good.

I want him to be inside all of me in a way that nothing can ever compare to. I want him in my cunt, in my ass. Fuck, I want him in my heart.

With a sudden hitched breath, I dropped onto him fully. Two thick cocks filled me simultaneously. Aearadan was in my pussy and my ass. Only a thin wall separated his girthy shafts. They pushed around inside of me, writhing and throbbing.

A masculine roar of pleasure erupted from his lips. His hips bucked and his tail rolled, thrashing in the shallow water. I watched his gorgeous abdominal muscles spasm with each sharp breath he took.

"Fuck, Aearadan, you're mixing up my insides. Gods, I'm so full of you." I ran my hand over the slight swell in my usually flat stomach. His cocks were so big, both swelling inside of me to a point that it extended my body. One could easily see his cock moving in my lower stomach as I rocked over his lengths.

More curses in his musical language spilled from his lips. Maybe it was a prayer. Words I didn't understand continued rushing from him as he marveled over the feeling of my warm, tight holes gripping both of his cocks. Aearadan had never felt such pleasure before, and I rejoiced in knowing that.

Despite the slight pinch of pain in my ass, I needed to move. I craved that euphoric release with Aearadan, and we would have it again. Carefully, to avoid ripping myself apart, I lifted myself.

Inflamed ecstasy rippled over my skin. Pure delight filled every nerve in my body with the sensation of Aearadan's firm, yet pliable, cocks moving inside me. Being doubly filled, the pressure was greater than before.

Electric tension sparked over my skin. It danced in the surrounding air, connecting us in a paradise of our own making. My flesh felt tight, and my nipples hardened into stiff peaks. As I sank down again, my head rolled back, making the length of my curly brown hair tickle my spine.

"Ah! Oh, gods. That feels so good. So good." Jumbled words and noises tumbled from me as I rode the merman to my heart's content. Rising and falling, I went slowly and cautiously at first. His slick cocks pressed into every nerve and sensitive place inside of my body, ensuring that I felt otherworldly pleasure with each lift and fall of my hips.

"Ah, Aearadan, I can feel you against my womb."

"Aearadan will fill Scylla womb someday. Fill to swell with life."

"Oh, gods." That threat, that promise, made my toes curl in the sand as I rode him harder.

"Aearadan put baby in Scylla." Something about those words made my brain utterly shatter apart. The ancient, animal promise of filling me in such a way that Aearadan alone would have that permanent mark on my body made me clench tighter on his members.

"Yes. Yes. Fill me. Fill all of me." An animal urge to be claimed by this man, this creature, had etched itself into my bones and now screamed to be set free. Some part of my brain told me that if Aearadan didn't claim my body and soul, then I would never be complete.

Lightning sparked around my body, shocking my flesh and nerve endings with the most scintillating sensations. Aearadan's clawed hands dug into my hips, holding me close as I rocked myself over his cocks. Each one moved inside of me with their own will, writhing and thrusting in a way that either my ass or pussy was always full.

Gods, so... so full.

I felt the seams of my being, like I was a doll, and soon I would burst from the forces yanking at me from all ends.

Bracing my palms on his hard chest, I glanced down to watch his beautiful green member disappearing inside of me. The multiple shades of green were lovely, but the sight of our combined fluids dripping out of me and coating his length sent my mind into overdrive. I was reeling from the erotic show and left wondering how that massive wriggling cock shoved itself inside of me each time I dropped my hips.

Suddenly, Aearadan flung his hands from my hips. I gasped as he curled his long arms around me and pulled me down to his chest. My breasts rubbed against his smooth, warm skin and something akin to a pleased purr flew from my lips.

I didn't recognize the wanton creature I was becoming with him - a version of me susceptible to pleasure, and eager to rejoice at the euphoria of it. It was a version of me I believed I could only be with Aearadan.

He grabbed my head, keeping one hand firm on my hip as I rocked on his cocks. His claws carefully scraped over my scalp, tangling into my hair to pull my face closer. I shuddered with the goosebumps rushing over my skin. Our lips locked and my insides quivered.

At the taste of my lips, Aearadan unleashed whatever control he'd been holding onto. His hips suddenly bucked. If not for his grip holding me flush to his body, I would have been sent flying.

He began thrusting up into me with more urgency. The tips of his claws grazed the skin on my hip to a near painful point, and with the fiery swell of another climax raging inside my core, I didn't care.

"Ah... Aearadan... I feel something coming again —"

"*Yes*," he growled. "*My Scylla will come.*"

I moaned, and he caught my bottom lip between his teeth. He sucked on my lip before releasing it to delve his tongue into my mouth. My clumsy tongue met his in kind while my hands scrambled all over his chest and shoulders to remain balanced.

His hard pounding and thick cocks curling inside of my tight walls made a taut cord inside of my body snap. I felt his members twisting and drilling inside of my pussy and ass, so large they rubbed everything. The string of heat holding me together ruptured apart, completely blowing me away.

Fluid gushed from me, the clear proof of my orgasm spraying over Aearadan's flexing abs. I broke away from his mouth, crying out as my shaking body seized up from the force of my climax. My muscles gave out, and I collapsed onto the merman.

Aearadan wasn't far behind. My pussy pulsed from the many waves of my release, squeezing his cocks. He groaned louder, pumping faster and faster until his cocks twitched inside of me.

He filled my cunt and ass with an intense spray of his cum, painting my insides with his permanent claim on me. There was so much of it that it instantly leaked out of my holes, escaping down his shafts with each slowing thrust. Our sticky fluids coated my thighs as he withdrew, leaving me leaking and gaping in his absence.

My body ached while satisfaction coursed through me. Legs wobbling, I fell over. Panting hard, I allowed Aearadan to pull me onto his warm side. Careful of the gills on his ribs, I snuggled into him. His seed continued leaking from me, but I'd take care of it soon enough.

Right now, I wanted to enjoy this elated, glowing silence with him.

Part Four

The silver orb in the sky hovered over the gently lapping waves of the inky sea. Its light glinted off the water, the only thing separating the endless black midnight sky from the dark waves.

I rested my exhausted body against the warmth of Aearadan. His arms curled around me, keeping me close as if we might merge into one being. Even when our hearts slowed, they remained in sync. Beating in time as if we shared one heart.

Heartsong.

It finally dawned on me what that meant.

What started as an ordinary day took a sharp turn into the extraordinary. My small, boring life where I'd begun to feel alone was now so much more. How could I go back to the lonesome monotony?

Despite my sated weariness, I abruptly sat up as my heart spiked with fear.

"Aearadan, thank you for saving my life." I gnawed on my bottom lip, wondering how to voice the thoughts building in my head. "But what now? This time with you has been amazing and I don't... I don't want to let you go."

I couldn't let him go. I knew I needed him. He'd

been watching over me, falling in love with me.

Aearadan sat up on his elbow. One long finger picked a piece of seaweed out of my hair. His handsome features became inexpressive as he vanished into his thoughts.

"What is my life to become now? Do I get a new boat and continue my life fishing while knowing something greater exists in the sea?" I swallowed over the rising tide of turmoil in my chest, raging like the ocean during a storm. "If my ancestor truly came from the sea, the ocean is in my blood."

"*Yes,*" he agreed. "*Ocean in your blood.*"

Aearadan's fingers moved from my hair to my cheek. My eyes closed as he held my face in one large palm. "*Aearadan not leave Scylla behind. Not supposed to fall in love with land people.*" He sighed. "*Scylla not land people. Scylla mine.*"

"So, what do we do?" The first tears spilled over my cheeks. The merman carefully swept them away with the pad of his thumb. "I hear the heart song Aearadan. Our song."

That's what the heartsong was. Not my lineage connecting me to the sea. It was my connection to him. To Aearadan.

When he'd claimed me, it went beyond the carnal attraction of two creatures entangled in the web of passion. It was a bond between our hearts that would last the rest of our lives.

"*Our song.*" His sea-blue eyes pierced my heart. "*Scylla want be with Aearadan?*"

Shifting onto my knees, I placed my hands

against his chest. "Yes! I do. If I could follow you into the sea, I would do so in an instant. I'd follow you into the ocean and never look back!"

As though he couldn't help himself, Aearadan launched forward. His mouth slammed into mine. However, this time there was no sweetness. This kiss wasn't tender and careful. It was rough and bruising. Enough that I whimpered, though I didn't pull away.

"*Scylla mine. Forever,*" he huffed against my lips, as out of breath as I was.

Then I felt the tingling in my skin. All over, it spread like a ticklish wildfire. Goosebumps dappled my skin, and the hair on the back of my neck rose. My blood simmered under my flesh.

Suddenly, I couldn't breathe.

My hands flew to my chest, pawing as I gasped at the dry air that did nothing for me. Nails dug into my skin, clawing up my throat as I fought for breath. My body fell back, writhing in the damp sand within the dark shadows of the cave.

Glancing everywhere, I frantically searched for Aearadan. Instead of seeing him in the dark, I felt his hands running over my limbs. His touch eased the strange pricking and shifting sensation in every visceral aspect of who and what I was.

"*Touch of magic. Reawaken the sea in Scylla blood.*" He sounded so very far away. "*Scylla need the water.*"

Lacking full awareness, I didn't know that Aearadan tucked me under his arm. I was too focused on my lack of air and itching skin.

Something under the skin on my back rose and my toes curled and stretched.

Something was happening to me.

Water splashed around us. It engulfed me entirely. Cold at first, my blood temperature rose to meet it, blanketing me with an internal warmth that fought off the ocean's nightly chill.

When I opened my mouth and gasped again, three slits flared open on the sides of my throat. Bubbles exploded from between my lips as I breathed, finally. This time, however, it was from the new gills on my neck.

Aearadan pulled us further from the shallows and into deeper water. His powerful tail flicked easily. We reached the heart of the cove in seconds. The spot where I'd spent years fishing my life away, waiting for the day something would change.

A line of frills breached my spine, growing along my back to my tailbone. More gills split on my ribs, and I breathed deeper. It settled the silent screaming in my instincts, telling me that this was real breathing.

My legs stayed separate, but my feet turned into frilled fins, like the end of Aearadan's tail. And where his smooth scale-like tail was as vibrant as emeralds, patches of silver scales formed along the sides of my legs and arms.

When I opened my eyes again, they were still brown, yet there was a new underlying silver tone made to absorb and catch light in the darkest depths of the oceans.

I wasn't the damsel meant to be saved from the sea. I was destined to be a part of it. My heart called to something, someone in the sea, and it always would.

Aearadan took my hand, smiling at me like he was seeing the sun for the first time. With his hand on mine and our song in my heart, I swam alongside him into the waves of my new future. A new life of love and treasure in the sea.

The End

Afterword

I wrote this short story for fun, and I hope everyone enjoys their time with it!

Again, special thanks to Anna Kate for her help cleaning this story up so I could share it!
You mean the world to me!

Books By This Author

Love & Monsters

On Your Knees

The Lost Omega

The Heat

In The Shadow Of Midnight

About The Author

Raven Flanagan

Mother, nerd, chaotic daydreamer.

Printed in Great Britain
by Amazon

26911341R00037